I was born in Portadown, Northern Ireland and entered the Nursing Profession qualifying as a State Registered Nurse.

After seeing a baby being born, I knew that Midwifery was for me, so travelled to Sheffield and Croydon to train. On qualifying, I practiced Midwifery throughout the country, finally arriving in Cay Maternity, Warneford Hospital Royal Leamington Spa, as a Midwifery Sister.

Eighteen months later saw me travelling to Australia to work, travel and camp throughout this massive continent before returning to Cay Maternity.

I later retired to Cornwall to enjoy the climate and to walk, play golf and Bridge.

THERE IS NONE SO QUEER AS FOLKS

Joan McCrory

THERE IS NONE SO QUEER AS FOLKS

Vanguard Press

VANGUARD PAPERBACK

A CIP catalogue record for this title is available from the British Library.

ISBN 9781784652012

Vanguard Press is an imprint of
Pegasus Elliot MacKenzie Publishers Ltd.
www.pegasuspublishers.com

First Published in 2017

Vanguard Press
Sheraton House Castle Park
Cambridge England

Printed & Bound in Great Britain

My grateful thanks to Mrs. Sandra Ann Patten, who with her computer skills, patience, tolerance and humour made life very bearable for me.

Thanks Sandra.

CATS AMONGST THE TOMBSTONES

It was a small village, with a population of four hundred people, lying in a sleepy valley away from the city lights.

Generation after generation of all the same families had lived here. Not many people left; fewer still came in to live.

Nothing unusual ever happened, except that the smell from the abattoir lingered over the houses now and then, when the wind was blowing in the wrong direction.

The pub, known as "The Thistle", was the centre of all communications and any evening you would find a large number of the men folk strolling along the main street towards it. The discussions and arguments about local politics drew them there like mice to cheese. Some revelled in telling tall stories and the whole spirit was one of merriment.

The women folk would meet during the day in the little post office cum supermarket and there seemed to be a well-recognised pecking order.

Mrs. Owen stood out as one of the "Important People" in the community. She was totally responsible for providing and arranging the flowers in the church, much to the annoyance of certain other ladies whose jealousy knew no bounds. They had, in good faith, offered their help as they felt they could share the burden but their overtures were firmly rejected.

It was Mrs. Owen who complained to the Vicar about the number of cats congregating in the graveyard and when Mrs. Owen complained, something had to done!

The Vicar being a kind, thoughtful and diplomatic man, had assured her that he and the Church Warden would look into the matter and reassured her that there was no need for her to worry.

In due course they inspected the cemetery and found no evidence of cats and no graves had been disturbed.

"Poor Mrs. Owen," sighed the Vicar. "She has not enough to do with her time. Maybe we could find something more for her."

The Church Warden, who was a man of few words, nodded his head in agreement.

Mrs. Owen whispered to her crony, Mrs. Bird, that there were quite a few cats in the graveyard. Mrs. Bird twittered to Mrs. Jackson, who ran the post office, that the graveyard was overrun with cats and she in turn told Mrs. Knew, the village gossip and the news travelled fast.

In no time at all the talk was of a plague of cats digging up the graves and eating the corpses. The village police constable, Joe Cartwright, was called in to investigate but he found nothing during a cold wet half hour spent amongst the dripping yew trees and headstones.

"A few cats around the place and they were all tagged," he growled to his wife. "It's a pity Mrs. Owen does not have enough to occupy her." As far as he was concerned, the matter was closed but not to Mrs. Owen.

She discussed the cats every day with the Vicar, who eventually addressed her in a stern voice and tried to suggest to her that it was all in her imagination.

Now, Mrs. Owen was a very large lady, with an over-bearing manner and she most certainly was not going to be put down by a timid man such as the Vicar. She snorted at him and continued to talk with her cronies, who gossiped to their husbands, who talked in the pub.

All pretty harmless nonsense.

Then like a bolt out of the blue, Mrs. Jackson went to see Joe Cartwright to report a missing person. Joe smoothed the pages of the Report Book on his desk and picked up his pen, thus prepared he looked at her.

"Who is missing, Mrs. Jackson?"

"Well, Joe Cartwright, let me tell you."

He raised his eyes to the ceiling and said "No doubt you will."

"Mrs. Kodack!"

"Mrs. Kodack?"

"Yes, and let me tell you, her husband is behaving in a most peculiar way." She nodded her head in a knowing manner.

He waited for her to go on.

"She's been gone for over two weeks and her husband is coming in to the house and closing all the curtains and…" She added triumphantly, "He spends all his time in the kitchen and there is the sound of sawing, not might I say, that I was being nosey but…"

He interrupted her, "What exactly does this mean, Mrs. Jackson?"

"Why, Joe," she exclaimed. "Between you and me, he's murdered his wife and he's the one feeding her to all those cats in the cemetery." Her face was alight with satisfaction.

"Is that all, Mrs. Jackson?"

The police constable was well aware of her dangerous weakness, in other words a tendency to mind other people's business and jump to conclusions. He surveyed her calmly. "Mrs. Kodack has not been reported missing by her husband." he explained.

"Of course not, if he's murdered her he's not going to report her missing is he." she answered airily.

"I'll look into it."

As she left the police station, Mrs. Owen was just passing.

"I've been to see Joe Cartwright" she explained, nodding her head to emphasise the news.

"Oh! About the cats?"

"No, about the murder!"

"What murder, Mrs. Jackson?" She asked looking covertly around the empty street, ensuring no one was at hand to hear what was being said. "Come home with me and we'll have a nice cup of tea and discuss it there."

"Oh yes, Mrs. Owen," agreed Mrs. Jackson. "People might hear us."

They walked, conspirators, but trying to appear as normal as their suppressed excitement would allow.

Police Constable Cartwright decided to make a call on Mr. Kodack. Knowing the gossiping women of the village, he knew to tread warily. He realised Mr. Kodack, being Polish and an outsider, made a comfortable suspect for them.

He arrived as the "Suspect" was arriving home from work.

"Just passing, Sir, thought I'd say hello."

"Hello, Constable, haven't seen you for quite some time, come inside."

Joe entered. “Missus away, Sir?”

“In Poland, Joe. Taking a few things to her relatives.” Was the calm reply.

“I should think you miss her?”

“Yes, but at present I am up to my ears in work. As you know, the abattoir is closing down this weekend for up-grading and I am busy sorting things out” he explained.

A tortoiseshell cat rubbed up against his leg and he picked her up. Stroking her head he asked ”Do you like cats?”

“Yes, Sir,”

“My wife idolises them. We have six in all but I don’t really mind as they replace the children we never had.” A shadow of sadness passed over his face.

“I must be going, Sir, nice to see you. Perhaps we could have a drink in the pub later.” suggested Joe.

“Sorry, Joe, work is my priority at the moment but soon though, soon.”

The police constable took his leave. He knew there had been no murder but after all, it was his job to check all the information given to him.

Mrs. Owen could hardly wait for her husband to arrive home before she was giving him the gossip. He being a timid little man listened to her story and as was his usual way said nothing.

That evening in the pub the men were talking about the “Murder.”

After grave discussion and a few rounds of drinks, someone suggested setting a trap for the “Murderer.” More discussion followed by more drinks and it was agreed to go to the graveyard and catch the villain.

It was a cold black windy night and of course to keep out the cold they carried a few bottles of spirits with them. Having decided to split into pairs they made themselves as comfortable as possible and sat behind the tombstones, where they lay in wait for the unsuspecting victim.

There must have been a dozen of them.

As the night wore on, an eerie silence fell over the cemetery. The darkness seemed to become darker and the cold, colder.

The courageous men shifted uneasily as nervousness brought on tension to the game but they drank from their bottles and kept their spirits up. Cold penetrated their coats and they shivered and drank some more. The air seemed alive with bats flying hither and thither. Creatures could be heard scurrying around them in the darkness. They huddled closer together and sought liquid comfort. In the stillness the crunch of a branch off a tree falling to the ground sounded like an explosion. Spines tingled and the hairs on the back of their necks stood on end. The bottles were completely emptied. It was the final straw when an owl hooted! The brave men from the little village took flight and in their panic, stumbled and fell to the ground remaining there until Joe Cartwright, the village policeman, found them later in a drunken stupor.

While this pantomime was taking place, Mrs. Kodack was at the final stages of her journey home. Eventually she entered her warm friendly house to find her husband in the kitchen cutting up meat.

"Not fit for human consumption," he explained when he had welcomed her. "The abattoir is closing for a few weeks so I thought this was the quickest way of getting rid of it," he pointed at the table.

"I've been cutting it into small pieces and feeding it to the stray cats in the graveyard. Thank goodness this is the last of it."

These days people are very slow to talk about the cats in the cemetery and "detective gossips" are not much heeded strangely enough… And the chat in the pub is more or less back to normal, although some men have difficulty meeting another's eye.

GHOST STORY

We had collected what seemed like thousands upon thousands of brochures promoting holidays in exotic locations. After perusal we argued, discussed and disagreed and in a final attempt to pacify everyone, my husband remembered a little fishing village where we had spent a lovely day, fishing, sunbathing and walking.

In the evening, we had gone to the local pub for a meal where the landlord had been very welcoming and his wife, Ivy, had gone to great extremes to make a "Special" for the worn-out children: sausage, mash and beans.

In fact, now when we talked about it, we remember we all had the same to eat but there had been a special magic in the air on that hot sunny evening.

We had always wanted to go back to this village and now here we were, arguing about the places where we wanted to holiday. After a long harrowing discussion, we did reach a unanimous decision to return to that small, quiet, some people would describe it as idyllic, fishing village on the east coast of Cornwall.

We always enjoyed Cornwall, with its secret sandy coves hidden away from the mainstream traffic. Where few people rarely parked their cars and walked for a short period before finding a narrow track, which would lead them down to the clean, white, sandy empty beaches we loved.

We loved the narrow winding lanes with the high flowering hedges, sometimes a nightmare when meeting other cars coming in the opposite direction. One then had to back up for a little way but everyone seemed to accept this situation with good humour and wave acknowledgement. How different this would have been in my home town.

A self-catering holiday in Cornwall was not so appealing! This was to be a family holiday for everyone, not merely the chosen few! As it turned out there was no need to worry! The car was packed with not an inch to spare. Surf boards, wind boards, wet suits, canoes and paddles, overflowed on to the roof rack. There was just enough room for all the passengers to squeeze inside. As with long journeys, we set off early in the morning in very high spirits. There was a lot of talk about surf boarding and canoeing and it seemed in no time at all we were on the motorway heading south towards sunny Cornwall!

The radio DJ kept up a continuous update on news, weather and travelling conditions. It was going to be a hot day he kept repeating and we all cheered but booed at the mention of traffic delays.

We stopped at service stations for short breaks and our children, Sandy and Jane, enjoyed their time playing computer games on the machines.

It was around three o'clock in the afternoon when we had left Taunton Deane Services behind, when there was a great bang and the car wobbled and my husband pulled it on to the hard shoulder. We all piled out to survey the damage. The front tyre was flat. The spare tyre, of course, was where we expected it to be, in the space especially made for a spare tyre with all our goods and chattels on top.

As with all good families we emptied out the neatly packed boot on to the hard shoulder. My husband Jeff set to change the tyre under the instruction of ten-year-old twins!

It was very hot and sticky standing on the hard shoulder. The DJ was proved to be correct with his weather forecast in fact, it was to be one of the hottest days of the year in more ways than one!

After cross words had been exchanged, the tyre was changed and all our essential goods and chattels were slung into the boot and the door banged closed.

Two very sullen, hot and irritable children sat in the back of a stifling hot stationary car, glaring at the back of the head of their dad, who wasted no more words and snapped his seat belt into place.

We slowly moved off into a heavy stream of traffic which had been building up whilst we were changing the tyre.

"Traffic jams building up on the M5 and A30." The DJ's voice was cut off in mid-stream as the radio was switched off!

We put Exeter behind us and our spirits began to soar once again.

A red oil alert light came on and the car was pulled off the A30 on to the hard shoulder. The bonnet was opened and a head disappeared and reappeared again in a moment. This was a job for those people in the yellow vans!

My husband set off to find one of those lovely little orange emergency telephones, which you rarely see when you need one.

As the sun beat down on us, the inside of the car was

becoming hotter by the minute. Windows were wide open but there was no movement of air and so we sat in pools of fluid, cooking like lobsters on a not to be forgotten memorable holiday.

The twins were hot, bored, tired and resentful at the break downs and had started rowing between themselves, when my hot and sweaty husband returned to the car.

It was the timing belt which had broken and we waited for help to arrive. A welcomed yellow van appeared with a smiling man who had come as quickly as he could but being at the height of our holiday season he had many emergency calls. In no time at all we were once more on our way.

Our disorderly children settled into what we always referred to as "an atmospheric mood" in other words you could cut the air with a knife!

It was the children who first saw the faded sign hidden by over-hanging branches.

Jeff applied the brakes and turned the car into the narrow winding lane, causing us to slide from side to side as though on a roller coaster.

The high hedges obliterated our view as we crawled round the twisting narrow corners, thanking God there was no on-coming traffic.

Another indistinct sign for the village pointed to an even narrower track which looked and felt as though few, if any, cars had ever driven along it.

The hedges were closing in around us scratching the paint work of the car. A sensation of panic was building up inside the airless car when a figure appeared in front of us.

He was a small, dark, black curly-haired bearded swarthy

character wearing brightly coloured pantaloons. His bare black hairy chest made him look like an ape but the large round dangling ear rings and black eyes gave him a look of a pirate.

In a blink of any eyelid he had disappeared. Our eyes were playing tricks on us, or maybe there was a fancy dress parade coming our way.

It was the children's voices breaking into our thoughts, questioning why the car was stopped, which caused my husband to shiver with fear.

We would have turned the car around if there had been room but we drove on and there in front of us was a granite cottage standing, like a sentinel, over-looking the sea.

The temperature in the car was dropping and everyone was closing the windows and pulling on their sweaters and cardigans and yet the sun was shining down on us from a cloudless sky.

The sleepy village straight ahead, with its half-dozen cottages and a few stationary cars, was bathed in sunshine and yet we were becoming colder and colder by the minute.

We all scrambled out of the car and stood by the gate surveying an over-grown path leading up to the cottage. There was little enthusiasm to run up the garden path. It would have been easier to have driven away and found overnight accommodation but we were mesmerised by the cottage and something beyond our control was willing us, like a magnet, towards the old oak door.

The owner of the cottage had given us instructions to pick up the key from underneath the mat and when we pulled back the old worn-out matting we found one enormous long, heavy, rusted key which must have lain there for centuries and had never been used. This key fitted the lock and with great force it turned making a hollow clunk. The door was jammed tight and with the aid of a shoulder pushing against it for several minutes it creaked open on its hinges and swung wide open.

A blast of icy cold sea spray slapped us in the face but when we touched them they were dry.

Foreign sounding voices shouted orders and we turned to look back the way we had come but we only saw our car sitting in bright sunshine. There was a boom as a cannon roared and the reek of gunpowder filled our throats and nostrils causing our eyes to water. Screaming voices reverberated in the cold dark abyss in front of us and the sound of sinking ships with cracking rigging seemed to come from afar. A stench of burning wood assailed our nostrils as we stood transfixed on the doorstep of the cottage. A great battle was taking place but we saw nothing. The "Pirate" with the brightly coloured pantaloons appeared before us swinging his cutlass from side to side, like a pendulum of a clock and as he brought the flashing steel in a sweeping arch towards us, we jumped backwards into the sunshine.

The door of the cottage closed silently behind us and we fled to our car and drove, as though we were pursued by the devil, to the nearest town where we stayed overnight.

At breakfast the following morning, two policemen with another man arrived at our table.

The stranger turned out to be the landlord, who called at the cottage to welcome us and to his horror found the cliff side had collapsed taking the cottage into the sea.

No one could throw any light on this extraordinary event and one could only assume that there had been a tremendous gale during the night which had swept the cliff and the cottage with it, into the sea. The villagers heard and saw nothing, we as a family said nothing.

The only thing that was found near the edge of the cliff was a very old rusty cutlass.

AN UNEXPECTED GIFT

The advert in the "Nursing Times" caught her attention. It was something different, a challenge, travel to a foreign country with all expenses paid and a very good salary included.

Sister Mary Jones had reached a crossroads in her nursing career. It was time for a change.

Writing her Curriculum Vitae was not a problem, or posting it to the address in Melbourne, Victoria, Australia.

It was two months later when the airmail letter arrived. Her heartbeat quickened with a suppressed excitement and with trembling fingers she opened the envelope. Inside was an airplane ticket for a flight to Melbourne and an added bonus of a cheque to cover any expenses incurred. The cover note was typewritten, brief and to the point.

All that was required from her was a phone call accepting the job and a date to commence her new post.

Her friends and colleagues came to Heathrow Airport, London and after kisses, cuddles and best wishes, they said their goodbyes and with a feeling of trepidation, she walked up the steps boarding the Boeing Jet 737 Quantas flight to Australia.

Mary decided to fly direct to Melbourne. The cheque she had received from her future employer had been banked and only what moneys needed she had withdrawn from her account. Her friends had teased her about being a miser in their opinion, she should be stopping for a few days en-route in different countries sightseeing. In her opinion, if the job was not to her liking, there would be enough coffers in the bank for her return journey.

The engines roared into life as she fastened her seat belt and the plane taxied along the runway, stopping at the end to turn facing the direction for take-off.

She felt the pulsation of the turbines and the thrust as her body was pushed into her seat as the plane soared, like a bird, skywards.

Awakening from a fitful sleep she glanced out of the window and had her first glimpse of Australia. A bright red ball of fire was rising over the Australian Desert, making her gasp at the breath-taking beautiful but fearful sunrise causing her a moment of panic. She was later to learn that the red of the desert reflect in the sun.

As the aircraft flew across the Australian Continent, she was in awe of the immenseness of this country. It was a few minutes before she was aware that the plane had landed and was taxiing along the runway towards its resting place on the hot tarmacadam.

Everything moved very quickly for her. One moment she was standing with her fellow passengers, holding tightly to her passport and the next she was being ushered outside by a tall, sun-tanned stranger, to a long grey limousine with black windows. Propped up in the back seat was a small hunchbacked elderly man with a face like a dried-up old prune. An ugly old man was her first impression, as his thin bony fingers reached out to take her hand in his. A smile of welcome swept across his features transforming his face into one of beauty. This little man was her employer and patient.

The journey to her new abode took just over two hours and during this period of time, Mister John, as he wished to be known, asked numerous questions about England. His England, as he called it.

In the early twenties when work was hard to find, his family emigrated to Australia from Kent. They had bought acres of land which they planted with apple and pear trees that they had brought with them, from there they had gone from strength to strength. Life in those days had been very tough and hard but they managed to survive the droughts.

He, being the only son, had taken over from his elderly parents and had built up an export and import business known world-wide.

He was now well and truly retired, with four wives behind him. His six sons; no daughters; with their wives, children and grandchildren, only visited him when he was on his deathbed.

A great sadness crept into his eyes as he mentioned his family and the zest for life, which had been present earlier in his speech, subsided.

Her duty as his personal nurse, was to inform his family when he became critically ill. Then the sky would darken, as the vultures came flocking in for the takings and with these words, Mister John fell asleep.

A cold shiver ran down her spine at his words and she wondered how often he had been critically ill. Mary was grateful for this moment when she could close her eyes and was awakened by the sound of voices and found they had arrived at their destination.

The house must have been beautiful in its earlier day, built in the old colonial-style period but now it had fallen into disrepair. Masonry from the parapet, lay untouched where it had fallen over the years. The rotten window frames looked as if the next storm would blow them from the casements and the grime on the glass was from want of cleaning. Two large Irish wolfhounds bounded out to greet them. A quiet word from Mister John sent them skulking back inside.

Mary turned to help her patient from the car, only to be pushed aside by the driver. She was to learn later that Jake, as he was known, was the driver, cook, butler and valet and had been with his master for forty years. He had drawn lines between her job and his job.

Mister John did not miss the smile of amusement flittering across her face and as their eyes met, a secretive grin passed between them and she knew she would be very happy nursing this humorous elderly gentleman.

Over the next few months, Mary and her patient grew closer together. She discussed several things outside her remit with him and he agreed with her suggestions. The rubble outside the house was removed. The windows sparkled inside and out. The decrepit kitchen with the now repaired water system, was shining with cleanliness and became the communal area where they ate their meals and swapped stories and relaxed together.

Mister John declared to all and sundry how wonderful it was to see the old house coming alive again. He, like his house, took on a new lease of life, supervising and re-planting some of his favourite plants and trees in front of the property.

John insisted they drop the "Mister" and when anyone called

him by his Christian name he was delighted.

It was Jake who congratulated Mary on making the remainder of his master's life enjoyable.

In the warm evenings, John, Mary and Jake sat together on the veranda, listening to John re-living his past. He talked about the balls, servants and friends and business acquaintances that came on horseback and stayed overnight. This was in the earlier days before the motor car. Finally, it was the airplane flying in and out. In this modern day, time meant money.

John was keeping well and he decided to go into Melbourne to transact business. Mary accompanied him with her bag of tricks, which held syringes and necessary drugs. His old friend, the oxygen cylinder, was his constant companion wherever he went.

Since her arrival, he had had two attacks when he would panic and she would calm and soothe him like a baby until the drugs took effect and he went to sleep.

Then came the rainy season when it rained down like stair-rods and the wet seeped in through every little crack and the house became oppressive. It seemed to be telling her something but she thought it was her imagination playing tricks on her.

John became critically ill.

Mary employed a team of nurses for around-the-clock nursing and she informed the relatives of John's critical state of health.

Mary had difficulty in sleeping and could be found sitting with Jake in the kitchen, drinking coffee until the early hours of the morning.

John made a slow recovery from his illness. How he had lived so long was indeed remarkable but as long as he had breath in his body he was going to enjoy life, especially now that he had at last found a suitable friend, nurse and someone who enjoyed his company.

It was a bright sunny morning when Mary went to awaken her friend and found he had gone to sleep forever. Jake was called and together they stood in silence remembering happier times.

The Doctor was notified of the death and when he arrived, he took Mary's hand in his own and spoke of the remarkable way she had lengthened John's life. She had given him the care, love and compassion which few were able to give.

Tears of sadness and grief rolled down her face at these words.

The last photograph placed inside her packed suitcase was of a small hunchback man, with a beautiful face and a mischievous smile in his eyes. In a strange way, John, in death, had won his last battle against his relatives.

She looked once more at the cheque made out to her for two million dollars and with a smile she tucked it inside her wallet.

ADULT TALK

The child saw the stick lying in the corner of the room. It was a walking stick, brown with a curved handle and a black rubber end. Her eyes opened wide in surprise and she smiled, her pleasure as she tiptoed away from the group of excitable adults to pick up the stick, allowing her fingers to caress the smooth shiny wood until her hands came to the well-worn handle.

In her mind she could still see her grandmother walking in the garden and she beside her, holding tightly to her hand, listening to her musical voice as they stopped at each flower bed, admiring the plants with the colourful flowers. Her grandmother loved her to ask the names of the shrubs and flowers and as she was a botanist by profession, it gave her great pleasure in sounding off the Latin names, followed by the more commonly known names. Every now and then, her grandmother would point her stick at an offending weed and she would kneel down and pull and pull, as she was instructed, until the weed, with its roots, was removed.

Her grandmother would mutter when she saw an area of garden where the one and only elderly part-time gardener had not found time to attend. This would distress her greatly and she would say "In my earlier years, before these old joints of mine started to ache, this garden was known as the 'Chelsea' of

Luddington" and then she would sigh deeply before moving on.

In her earlier days, Grandmother, with the help of her then younger part time gardener, had spent many, many happy hours together planning, organising and re-planting when sometimes shrubs were planted in the wrong area of the garden. Always weeding and pruning until perfection was reached and then a little weed would point upwards out of the soil and she would roar like a lioness in pain until the gardener arrived to be confronted by a very angry woman waving the offending weed.

It was a long time ago when Grandfather died. Mummy said he died in the war but which war? She never asked but she did hear her Mum say to her Dad, "A pity she never married again."

Then they would both laugh as though they knew something secret about Grandmother. When asked it was always the same answer. "Adult Talk."

Tommy, the elderly part-time gardener, was about Grandmother's age and had been working here from the day Grandmother and Grandfather moved into this house.

If we, Mum or Dad and I, arrived unexpectedly to visit, Tommy was either in the garden or in the house. We always knew when he was in the house because his gardening boots would be outside the back door. If we visited in the evening, Tommy would be dressed in his best outfit sitting contentedly smoking his pipe, in what was known as Grandfather's chair. He would make some excuse and leave us. We saw him later when he thought we had gone, making his way back to the house. Then Mum and Dad would burst out laughing and still they never shared their joke with me. Adults do behave oddly.

She wondered dreamily whether or not she could keep this walking stick of Grandmother's because Grandmother would not need it any more.

It was the sound of the car on the gravel outside, then the sound of voices and the slamming of car doors, which aroused her from her reverie. She placed the stick back into its corner position and sidled back to her mum. The lounge door opened and in walked her grandmother followed by Tommy, the part time gardener "dressed to kill" as my mum would say.

Grandmother looking tall and elegant and so much younger spotted me, shyly holding my mum's hand.

"It's wonderful what a hip replacement can do for you," she proudly exclaimed to the waiting relatives, "and, Gloria, come and meet your new Grandfather."

THE MAGICAL GLEN

Very few people had ever seen him, in fact, very, very few people had ever seen him but they knew he was there. He looked just like you'd expect, with his forest-green tunic, long green tights and a neat green hat which came to a point, with a red magical tassel which flopped on to his left shoulder. Of course he also wore a red belt with a huge golden buckle which also held wonderful magical powers.

Fergal the leprechaun watched over his Glen and protected it in every way you could imagine. He loved to care for the wild animals which lived in the woods. In the spring when the birds were nesting, he would cast a magical circle around the woods to keep the wild cats and pet cats out, so that they would not harm the baby birds. Because the birds felt so safe and happy, they sang at the top of their voices all day and that was why the woods in the Glen were called "The Musical Woods."

One of Fergal's other jobs was to care for the trees and plants. After a storm, he would check every tree and if any had been blown down he would use his magic buckle to put the roots deeper into the soil and the tree would grow again. Snowdrops and bluebells carpeted the floor of the woods and wild orchids peeped out of all sorts of nooks and crannies. Besides the song of the birds, the other sound the little leprechaun liked best, was the sound of the river tinkling over the pebbles and splashing from the rocks as it rushed through the trees, merrily making more music on its way down to the sea. When the salmon came up the river to spawn, it was a very busy time for Fergal, he made sure they arrived safe and sound at the very spot where they had begun their lives. Later he guided the tiny new salmon back down to the sea, where they would grow large and strong and in their turn, return to the river when they were old enough.

His reward for all this work was very special. He would take off the heavy red belt with its gold buckle, lay it on a lovely soft grassy place and lie on it. You are wondering what is so special about that! When Fergal lay on the belt he and it disappeared from sight for a short while but he could still hear all the wonderful sounds around him; the birds singing their songs, the trees rustling their leaves to the tune, the river tinkling more loudly and the frogs croaking their own strange sounds. Occasionally, Fergal and the frogs would dance to the music while the rabbits, squirrels and deer looked on.

Because everyone knew about the magic in the Glen and didn't quite know what to make of it, very few people ever visited it.

One glorious summer's day, Fergal, who was sunbathing under a large toadstool, whose shadow kept the sun out of his eyes, felt vibrations. Very strong vibrations, as if a herd of cows were charging through the Glen. He jumped to his feet and fastening his broad red belt and putting on his cap, tilted his little head and listened very carefully. The sounds of the voices of humans came to him on the wind and the trees cried out in pain and moaned with grief as their branches were torn off.

Birds panicked and flapped about all over the place making their warning calls. Rabbits playing outside their burrows froze with fright for a second or two and then disappeared down them in a flurry of white tails, feet and dust. Ears pricked, the deer bounded away from the danger and squirrels fled up to the highest branches of the trees.

Three young boys came rushing amongst the trees chasing each other, destroying the quietness with their loud shouts and trampling thoughtlessly on the beautiful flowers, ripping twigs and branches from the trees. Fergal, watching unseen, could hardly believe his eyes. He certainly could not understand the needless destruction.

The boys threw the branches into the fast flowing water by running alongside the bank and throwing stones in great excitement. The grasses and mosses felt their heavy feet and shrank lower to the ground. The boys did not know that they were running thoughtlessly and very quickly towards the bog.

The Bog knew they were coming. It could feel its lunch approach and with every step the boys took towards it was more and more prepared for the meal. That was the way the Bog thought about careless people and animals who came within its clutches. The green moss moved silently, making the river bank seem safe to walk on, hiding the treacherous, dangerous Bog beneath.

Fergal had been kept quite busy putting right, with his magical buckle, the damage they had caused but he heard their screams of terror as the Bog took hold of their feet and legs and began to suck them down and down. It only took a second of his time to come to them. Then they were struggling and shouting and trying to pull each other out but the more they struggled the more the Bog drew them in, until they were almost up to their armpits.

Fergal being a polite leprechaun, who never interfered in anyone else's business, watched as the boys tried to escape and then he asked in his strange high-pitched voice if they needed any help. The boy's eyes flew wide open in amazement and they thought they were seeing and hearing things. The Bog knew the voice and began to suck faster and faster, trembling with rage, for it knew from past experience that Fergal didn't like it to devour people and animals and had robbed it of a number of meals. The boys squealed their answer, terrified. In a moment, Fergal had undone his broad red belt with the large golden buckle and began to swing it round and around. As it whirled, the large golden buckle gleamed in the sunlight and the belt began to get thinner and thinner and longer and longer until it became a lasso. Removing his green cap with the big red tassel he fastened it to the lasso and once more swung it around over his head. When he was satisfied that everything was flying perfectly he let go and it flew over the heads of the boys and settled around their shoulders. Fergal then gave his instructions. The boys put their arms through the loop and the green cap, with its magical red tassel, flew upwards tightening the belt and pulling them straight up into the air. It shook them gently to get rid of some of the mud from their clothing and slowly set them down on firm dry land, well away from the disappointed Bog, which moaned and complained and made sucking noises for a very long time.

Fergal went to the boys but before removing the red belt with the magical golden buckle and the wonderful cap with the red tassel, he made them promise two things.

One was that they must never tell that they had seen him and this was followed by a very serious account of what would happen to them if they did!

The second promise, I think you know what that must be.

MISTAKEN IDENTITY

Peggotty, my ageing grey nosed black Labrador, with her arthritic joints, was accustomed to going for her first walk of the day early in the morning. She was not as sprightly or high-spirited now that she was older and to walk short distances was her limit.

Her tailed wagged furiously as the door of the lounge was opened and we stepped onto the patio. Stopping for a few moments surveying the world, with her nose in the air snuffing in the beautiful scents and I checking that the heron had not visited for his breakfast before going on his way. The netting that had been placed over the pond appeared to be a life saver, as the numbers of brightly coloured fish swimming in and out of the reeds were intact.

Walking down the garden to open the gate into the field, Pegs, as she is commonly known, brushed past my legs in her enthusiasm to waddle on to her beloved pastures.

The sky was blue and cloudless and the view across the fields showed the river sparkling in the sunshine and the cows in the distance munching on grass contentedly. It was going to be another hot sunny day.

Pegs walking at her leisurely pace, stopped now and then to sniff out the different scents and followed mysterious trails, suddenly started barking. She jumped backwards and forwards head on one side with ears cocked and tail wagging creating enough noise to awaken the dead, never mind my neighbours asleep in their beds. When called “Come” she continued with her game, occasionally rolling on her back waving her legs in the air. This was magic! My staid old pet had been turned into a rejuvenated dog. There was something in the long grass which she found to her liking, causing her such frivolity.

Again, ordering her to “Come”, Pegs once again disobeyed me and continued with her activities. Now she laid full length on the ground as flat as she could spreading herself out, head resting between her front paws, staring as though trying to hypnotise her find, ears cocked and tail swinging back and forth like a pendulum on a clock. Walking back to her in the long grass, curled up into a tiny ball, was a small hedgehog. Pegs growled as she defended her “Find”. Carefully picking up the little animal and placing him in the palm of my hand, he looked even smaller sitting there. He was three to four inches long and his spines were soft and covered in a grey down as though a giant spider had covered him with its web. His eyes remained unopened, he was very immature.

The cattle were munching their way slowly but steadily towards us and if he were in the grass he would be trampled to death. The decision was made, so with the little creature held safely and gently in my hand with Pegs bounding backwards and forwards with her head held high and tail raised like a ship in full sail, we returned home. Placing the hedgehog on the lawn safely, it was time to telephone the local vet for advice and he implied that the immature hedgehog had little hope of survival.

Looking out into the garden was a pleasant surprise to see Cedric the hedgehog, a name I decided upon, toddling along, with Pegs bringing up the rear guard heading for the edge of the lawn. Pegs was taken by surprise when her "baby" went tumbling over the edge into the flowerbed but as quick as a flash she picked him up and carried him into the centre of the lawn where she sat him down gently. She started to lick him all over as a mother with her puppy. Poor Pegs, her maternal instincts were aroused.

Cedric did not seem to mind the attention but when Pegs stopped he was off again. This time, Pegs nosed him towards a flat end of the lawn where he foraged under the rose bushes, whilst the very proud adopted mother sat overseeing her little charge.

Placing a saucer with a little water on the lawn, Cedric was picked up and placed feet first into it. Whether or not he drank, there was no sure way of knowing but he enjoyed the experience of paddling in it. Pegs watched the antics of her baby for a few minutes, before picking him up by the scruff of his neck and licking him clean.

The main problem was how to feed this tiny creature, so setting out in pursuit of a nice fat juicy slug; cutting it into tiny pieces; it was placed beside Cedric. He nosed around it but did not eat. Pegs sniffed around these little pieces and showed her distaste by scratching them into the flower border and covering the slug with soil. Picking up her charge she stalked back to the rose bushes depositing Cedric on the decaying leaves. The vibrations from Pegs, was to leave it to the animals!

As day turned into night, it was time to consider where to bed, Cedric. As the compost heap was one of his many haunts and a safe haven for a baby hedgehog, he was settled in clean straw and we returned indoors for the remainder of the evening but it was not very long before Pegs started whining and barking at an intruder outside. On opening the door she swept, like a tornado, into the darkness to the fish pond where she continued barking. This time her message was received and so the investigation began.

In the pond swimming for his life was Cedric. He had managed to fall through the netting covering the pond. Fishing the bedraggled little fellow out of the water and inspecting him from snout to tail his midnight swim had done him no harm but after that drama he was taken into the house for the night.

Two of his nine lives had been spared by a very diligent and devoted dog. As Pegs cleaned her charge, a cardboard box was found and lined with felt and under the watchful eye of Pegs, her "baby" was tucked in for the night. In the morning, Pegs was lying on her side and snuggled up against her belly curled up in a little ball was Cedric.

Over the next few weeks, Cedric was steadily growing and his eyes were now open and clear and his spines were hardening. The grey down had disappeared or was licked off by Pegs and soon he would be on his way to find a lady friend. Pegs was unaware that her friend was maturing and when there was a distinctive yelp, Pegs had lifted Cedric for the last time. She came to me with her tail tucked between her legs and her head drooped. With a little difficulty opening her mouth and inspecting inside there was little damage to be seen. Pegs had learned her first painful lesson. Her friend had some very formidable spines and must be left alone. It was shortly after this incident when Cedric disappeared.

Pegs was frantic when she could not find him. She searched under the rose bushes and turned the compost heap upside down but there was no sign of him. She sniffed and searched the field but Cedric was gone. Every day Pegs continued her search.

Autumn turned to winter and spring appeared but Pegs continued with her crusade. It was nearly a year since Cedric had entered our lives and departed unexpectedly, when Pegs trotted off on her regular search of the garden. Her first stop, always, was the compost heap. She had grown older and had lost her new found youthfulness.

Imagine my surprise when hearing her familiar excited barking and looking out into the garden saw her playing. She was jumping backwards and forwards, tail wagging, ears cocked and head on one side.

In her excitement she rolled on to her back waving her legs in the air and then stood up shaking herself as though awakening from a wonderful dream. Then she ran. Like the wind, towards me, barking and running back to the compost heap. Something was amiss, following her, I found emerging from the mass of grass cuttings, a hedgehog with her young family. "Cedrica" had returned.

CLEAN SWEEP

The emaciated woman with a hawk-like face stared into the mirror. She patted her black dyed hair into place and nodded with satisfaction at her reflection. She looked around the bedroom and observed a few stray black hairs on the dressing table. Pulling a tissue from its box, she deftly picked up the rubbish and carried it to the en-suite bathroom, where she watched it swirl in the flush pan until it disappeared.

She checked that the bathroom was scrupulously clean before making her way downstairs and with a routine of years, her small glittering eyes darted from left to right missing nothing in their scrutiny.

Her whole face glowed with happiness as she viewed her lounge. Her heart swelled with pride as she surveyed the beauty she had created around herself.

Visitors were never encouraged into her house, because she could not bear to see her precious carpet smudged by dirty shoes, nor her exquisite cushions creased when sat on.

Then she thought, at last, unwillingly, about her husband and how soon her happiness would evaporate on his return home. She would become agitated and her palpitations would begin. He took away all the pleasure that she derived from this perfection but she took comfort in the thought that one day, not far in the future, she would be rid of this man.

Fluffing up the cushions one more time before placing them in their strategic places on the settee, she walked into the kitchen, hastily closing the door to prevent the smell of cooking from permeating the house.

The kitchen sparkled like diamonds in the light. When she noticed that the water had boiled over on to her shining clean stove, she pursed her lips in annoyance. This must have happened when I answered the telephone, she thought, as she quickly tore some pieces from the roll of paper towels, which cleverly matched the kitchen tiles, and mopped up the spillage. In future she decided she would not allow any distractions when cooking: she would unplug the telephone.

Cooking was her pet hate because her mirror like, glittering saucepans became soiled and it took ages to restore them to their pristine state. When draining the vegetables into her gleaming sink she would feel the rapid beat of her heart and her body would tremble with apprehension but this had been overcome by straining the vegetables directly into the water drain outside. Her husband had not agreed to this procedure because he thought it was not hygienic but in the end she had her way.

In the dining room everything sat in exactly the same place as it had occupied since they had first come to live here. The table was covered with a clean crisp white tablecloth and the silver, cleaned daily, shone brightly in the light. Walking around the table she inspected the two settings closely.

The grandfather clock boomed out six times and on the last stroke she heard him enter the house. The front door slammed and she jumped, just as she always did.

"Why do you slam the door every time you come in?" She greeted him sharply.

"Oh. Do I?" His voice was mildly tinged with irritation.

"I have told you time and time again and you don't listen".

She did not notice that she wrung her hands in her deep agitation.

"Yes, dear." The inevitable response and in his preoccupation he did not notice her distress, or else he had become so accustomed to the performance that it failed to register.

"You're wearing your shoes." Her voice rose and her eyes bulged with disbelief.

"Yes, dear." The newspaper was opened and he immersed himself in the evening news.

Over the past ten years her hatred had been slowly and steadily building up inside her. Now she surveyed him coldly, no warm feelings survived. It hardly crossed her mind to wonder if they had ever existed.

"You never appreciate what I do for you."

"Yes, dear." He was engrossed in his paper.

Bringing his slippers, she changed his shoes, taking them out to the utility room, where she placed them on to brown paper, always brown paper, newspaper soiled her work surfaces. With the dustpan and brush she proceeded to eliminate his trail to the front door removing every trace and mark, real and imagined, from the carpet. After emptying the polished dustpan into the dustbin, she once more went to her husband.

"Why do you always throw your overcoat over the sofa, there is a cloakroom." Her rage welled up inside her. The thin lips tightened as picking up the coat she marched to the cloakroom and emptied the pockets, reading the contents, before returning to the dustbin with the items which she deemed to be rubbish.

The meat was overdone and the vegetables soggy but she served the meal on to two cold plates before scrupulously scrubbing the saucepan.

He took a mouthful and grimaced at the unpleasant flavour.

"Something wrong?" Her lips broadened with a peculiar smile, which seemed to invite him to the mistake of making a comment.

"No, dear". He answered swiftly, swallowing the cold food. Almost before the last morsel had passed his lips, she was on her feet picking up their plates and taking them to the kitchen to be washed, dried and placed in a cupboard. When this had been done, dessert was served and the whole routine was repeated relentlessly.

He sighed as he left the table and escaped to his newspaper. He would not see his wife again. She would remain to clean the kitchen and then the lounge after he had retired for the night. His thoughts went back over the years he had been married. He had never slept with her, not even on their short honeymoon. If it had not been for meeting Christine, he supposed he might have gone mad. "Meeting Christine" hardly described the event. He had literally bowled her over as he rushed out of the office on his way to lunch, just a few weeks after returning from his honeymoon. By way of apology he had invited her to join him. As they talked they found they were relaxed together and their meetings became frequent. Eventually they made love.

When he had explained about his marriage, Christine had asked him about divorcing his wife but he had refused. His wife, as he had explained, was a very wealthy woman and on his small salary he would never be able to support any woman but if something happened to her then he would be very well off indeed. The matter was never discussed again.

The next morning, snow lay on the ground and as he cleared a path to the drain he noticed the large stones by the back door. They were the leftovers from the rockery that he had been building in the summer. He stacked them very neatly before going into the kitchen for salt to sprinkle on the cleared path. His wife seeing the trail of snow on the kitchen floor screamed her abuse at him, shouting that in future she would clear the path.

He had gone to work wondering how long this marriage would last.

There were intermittent snow falls and severe frosts all week. The roads and paths had become ice rinks but his routine continued. He appeared to be more preoccupied than usual; she carried on with her unvarying tasks.

He stood in the hall, gathering all the courage he could muster. He had made his decision and he wanted a divorce. There was no sound. Shrugging his shoulders he advanced into the lounge to find his wife awaiting him. He immediately made the announcement he had rehearsed over and over again on his way home.

Her lips broadened with her smile and she calmly replied, "Yes." Her eyes did not smile.

His face registered shock. His jaw dropped and an incredulous expression passed over his face.

"Did… you… say… yes?" he stuttered.

"Yes I did. Tonight you can serve dinner." and with no more

ado she turned on her heels and walked tall into the dining room where she sat at the table and waited.

He quickly recovered from the shock and hastily removing his coat and carefully hanging it in the cloakroom he almost danced into the kitchen. It was unbelievable. She had said "Yes!"

A great surge of happiness filled his heart and the burden of all those miserable years was lifted. The relief that poured through him at the knowledge that he would no longer have to go through the unbearable ordeal night after night made him breathless. His heart pounded with his excitement and his spirits were lifted to a peak of utter euphoria and joy. Suddenly he felt as if his chest were being crushed by steel hands. He could hardly breathe, the severe pain caused him to cry out before crashing into oblivion.

She heard the noise and strolled into the room. Blood had spattered over the floor where he had hit his head on the sink unit before he had collapsed to the floor. Tearing off pieces of paper from the roll she mopped up the sticky red mess. Not one glance did she give to the prostrate figure.

Picking up the saucepan from the stove, as was her usual custom, she stepped over the body and walked out on to the path that glittered with thick impacted ice. Her feet slipped and skidded and as she tried to regain her balance she threw her precious saucepan away from her and it rocketed down the path. The lid spun through the air like a capsule from outer space. Her high-pitched scream seemed to echo around the garden as her head smashed against the neatly stacked stones outside the back door.

THE CREATURES FROM THE BLACK DEPTHS

The village, known as Gurnard, in its heyday, had been a thriving, busy fishing port but it had floundered and the young folk had left to find work in other places.

Now it consisted of two dozen granite houses, a church, a shop-cum-post-office and a dilapidated petrol station. "The Pit" was the local pub where all the men, with the exception of Ken Pratt and his son, Stephen, gathered in the evening to sit and talk of better days.

Derelict buildings were dotted around the landscape and the wharf had fallen into disrepair. Danger notices appeared at intervals along the neglected areas. Debris, washed in by the tides over the years, had accumulated in the channel, causing navigational difficulties for the two small boats that went fishing daily. The catches were small and the villagers bought them. There was no need these days for refrigerated lorries to call and collect for the cities.

Over the past years, Father O'Leary, the local priest, would bless the fishing fleet and different species of fish. These were put back into the sea alive, but in spite of it all, the fishing industry had ground to a halt.

The superstitious people of this village were convinced they knew the reason for the collapse of their once thriving industry, or so they thought! It had to do with the inhabitants on the island.

The rocky barren island was approximately one mile from the main land and occasionally a fishing crew would place a few lobster pots in the vicinity and collect them on their return from fishing but on this occasion Ken Pratt and his son, Stephen, for some unknown reason had sailed directly into port and unloaded the fish. After swabbing the deck of the boat they had then gone to the "The Pit" to have a few drinks. Coming out of the pub Ken and his son, decided to take the rowing boat and bring in the lobster pots.

It was a beautiful evening and the sun was setting as they rowed towards the island. They began pulling up the pots and each one held a lobster but it was when they came to the last pot that Ken saw the creatures coming out of the sea. He froze in his seat and his eyeballs nearly popped out of their sockets with shock. His son, on seeing his father's expression, turned and looked in the same direction. He shook with fear as he saw the black creatures with bulging eyes and large protuberances on their backs. The monsters had great difficulty scrambling up on to the rocks. Ken and Stephen saw their webbed feet.

By now it was dark and in their panic to escape they had great difficulty in putting the oars in to the rowlocks but after several attempts they rowed as though chased by the devil, back to the shore, leaving the last lobster pot behind. Beaching the boat they raced to the pub.

The merriment and talk instantly ceased as the two men collapsed on to a seat. It was obvious to all that something dreadful had happened.

"Bring brandy," yelled one fisherman.

"What's happened, Ken?" Asked another and before long they were encircled by their comrades. After several brandies, Ken Pratt began telling his story.

This was too much for the superstitious men, they laughed and jeered and made mock of the two petrified fishermen.

"You've had too much to drink." They laughed but it was the sound of forced laughter.

This became a standing joke in the village and whenever Ken and Stephen, walked down the main street they heard the snide remarks and from then onwards they held themselves aloof from the villagers and never went back to the pub.

It was a source of conversation, as every evening, the fishermen, with the exception of Ken Pratt and his son, visited the pub but it was noticeable that lobster pots had never been placed near the island from that night onwards.

Even the reduced catches of fish began to dwindle and one of the fishing fleet mentioned this matter in the pub.

"Probably the island creatures are devouring the fish," this was said as a joke but very few men laughed. There appeared to be a tension building amongst them.

It was John Hanson, the "bravado" of the village who boasted that he would go to the island and see what was happening but he was advised against it. However, he took his rowing boat, under the cover of darkness, out into a heavy sea swell. His body was found the next day washed up on the beach. The local people said he had died of fright as he had a look of horror on his face. From then onwards, the fishing boats made a detour away from the island when they went to sea.

The catches got smaller and smaller.

It was generally thought at the time that the black creatures living on the island had enormous appetites. There was no other obvious reason, or was there? Could it be that the enormous amounts of fish taken over the years had never given them time to replenish.

Every day, the men, with their wrinkled weather-beaten faces, sat outside their cottages dressed in their woollen sweaters, heavy trousers and sea going boots, smoking their pipes and talking of better days. Their wives occasionally joined them, clicking their needles as they knitted and nodding their heads in agreement.

Joe Griffin, the eldest villager, always told the story of the day when his boat was so loaded with fish, that he thought it would sink as it lay so deep in the water, they had limped into the quayside and it had taken hours to unload.

Ay, yes, those were the days! They puffed on their pipes and their eyes were filled with a melancholy.

One bright sunny day, as these men sat outside their little cottages, on the hill overlooking the wharf, a large lorry rattled over the cobbled stones down the main street to the quay. It had been many years since a strange lorry, or for that matter a vehicle of any description, had arrived in the village, except for the lorry that brought provisions and post for the shop-cum-post-office.

The men looked at each other with a mixture of curiosity, bewilderment and a little fear showed in their eyes. Some, in fact, had shaken their heads in disbelief.

"Strangers in the village, no good will come of this," one muttered and every one grunted in agreement.

Ken Pratt with his son, sat aloof from them as usual thoughtfully viewed the lorry. Ken was able to read most of the information on the side of the vehicle as it passed "Training School for Under Water..." but he kept this information to himself.

The driver of the lorry parked it on the quayside and remained inside. No one from the village went near.

It was in the evening when Ken Pratt and Stephen, strolled down the hill and entered the pub. A curious silence descended as Ken ordered two pints of beer. Father and son went and sat in a corner, away from the entrance to the pub and waited patiently.

It was soon after this event when Joe Griffin took his old labrador, Jess, for her last walk prior to retiring, for his evening beverage at "The Pit."

The sun was setting and the darkness was closing in, when Joe stared out to sea. He thought he saw something moving in the water and looked again. He could not believe what he saw. The black heads and black humps of the sea monsters were swimming directly to the quayside. Dropping the dog's lead, he took flight and he ran as though the devil himself was trying to catch him. Rushing into the pub, falling on to the nearest seat he gasped and stuttered his news. The village was being invaded by the sea creatures.

Faces paled and in the silence you could have heard a pin drop. Then everyone started talking at once and their panic stricken voices could be heard in the main street. A sudden silence descended when Ken Pratt and his son, Stephen, rose from their corner seat. Eyes, with an expectant look in them, stared at Ken Pratt but the only words Ken spoke was, "Good Night."

THE MYSTERY MAN

Helen Johnson and her friend Julia Ambrose rested their arms on the rails of the ship which had berthed in Sydney for passengers to disembark and re-embark. They were returning to England having worked for the past three years in Australia.

It was a very enjoyable pastime surveying the newcomers, with their colourful garlands around their necks and tear-stained faces struggling with their suitcases up the gang plank.

The two young women would speculate on who they were and to which trade or profession they belonged. Usually they had jumped to the wrong conclusion but it was fun.

The quayside was teeming with people of all nationalities, pushing and shoving, forwards, backwards and sideways. Heads bobbed up and down like corks in a bath full of water, as friends became separated in the masses and were trying to make visual contact. It was complete chaos.

The colourful bunting hanging from every nook and cranny flapped in the sea breeze as the bandsmen, in their scarlet tunics and dark trousers, played a melody of tunes which could just be heard above the deafening mayhem.

It was Julia, who noticed the unkempt man, in his early forties, moving up the gangplank. He walked with an air of self-confidence and his luggage was a small holdall. She shouted above the noise to her friend drawing her attention to him. She glanced in his direction, shrugged her shoulders and lost interest but Julia continued to observe him until he disappeared down a stairway.

A disturbance of the quayside caused both women to shake their heads in bewilderment, as a twelve-year-old boy snatched an elderly lady's handbag and tried to make off with it. What hope had he of escaping! He was penned in by the crowds. The handbag was returned to the owner and before their boggling eyes the boy was manhandled like a sack of potatoes over the heads of the people to what looked like a man in uniform, possibly a policeman.

The ship's siren sounded three times. A hush fell over the crowd and the clanking of the anchors was heard as they were drawn up. The band played the haunting melody "Will ye no come back again" as the ship pulled away from the quayside.

People waved, cried, shouted and threw streamers to the departing passengers.

It was always a brief and sad moment when they cruised off for distant land; in this case the next stop was Acapulco, Mexico; leaving behind friends, relatives and families.

Julia and Helen remained on deck for a very long time after the other passengers had dispersed, watching the land slowly disappear from view thinking of their friends far away in Australia.

The unkempt man had seen the tall, slender young woman with the piercing blue eyes watching him as he came on board. He smiled inwardly when he thought of the disappointment ahead of her. Once he told her he was penniless she would ignore him, like so many women before. José Hernandez was an extraordinary man who had been born into poverty and he had found early in his young life that he had one skill. With a touch of determination and perseverance, he honed and refined it until he became one of the most famous glassblowers in Acapulco, fighting his way into a world of hard cynical business men and succeeding where others had failed.

Now with several factories across the world, producing anything from a glass trinket to armoured plating, a yacht moored in Acapulco Bay, a 737 Boeing Jet and a beautiful residence dominating the city where he, his wife and two daughters lived. He was a millionaire many times over. If asked he had no idea of how much he was worth financially but he knew how to apply his wealth to caring for his family.

He had built a villa for his parents outside the city and his money had paid for the education of his three brothers, who were now directors in his businesses. José's family took precedence over everything.

His mouth filled with distaste when he thought back over the past three months. Sitting in his office, browsing through the annual reports from his industries, he had noticed that one small factory on an island had significantly higher profits than any other. His gut feeling told him that something was terribly wrong and he had decided to investigate the matter, not as the owner but as a highly competent glassblower.

What he found was alarming. The peasant workers were horribly exploited, working fourteen hour shifts per day and receiving only a pittance, hardly enough to feed and clothe them.

The day of reckoning was arriving for his management team and they had no inkling of it.

The holdall was filled to capacity, not with clothing, but paper; his reports, recommendations and final analysis of his fact finding mission.

As was the custom on board ship, everyone dressed for dinner.

The two friends were dressing when Julia casually mentioned the unkempt stranger saying it would be exciting if he were sitting at their table. Helen, in her usual sarcastic manner replied that he would never get in for dinner if those were the only clothes he possessed.

To Julia, the mention of clothes was like a red rag to a bull, they held little importance in her life style as she loved meeting people from all walks of life. You couldn't be a slave to fashion and use it as a measure of a person's "worthiness" if you wanted to meet the range of people that Julia did. This particular stranger intrigued her, so much so, that she had gone to see her good friend the Catering Officer to explain that she would like him seated at their table. She was pleased with herself when she went in to dinner to find him sitting where she expected him to be. Of course she feigned surprise. It was her little secret. Wine, as usual, was ordered and when the two glasses were filled and the waiter had gone, Julia picked up the bottle and offered José some wine. This was his opportunity to explain that he was penniless and could not afford to return the compliment, at which, Julia simply burst out laughing, apologised and insisted that if he were sitting at their table he most certainly must enjoy their wine.

It was obvious to him that he would not win this argument so he conceded the point with good grace. Glancing at his tattered clothes and at the elegant women across the table he concluded that she was a great puzzle to him. He had difficulty coping with her generosity towards him. By the end of the journey he would begin to realise that there were still compassionate people around.

The more he met up with these two young women the more he relaxed and enjoyed himself for the first time in years. These two women required nothing from him except his company and he found this exceptional behaviour.

At the end of the enjoyable meal, Helen asked him if he was going to dance. He shook his head and replied in the negative, catching Julia's eye, he thought he saw disappointment, or was it his imagination but she only smiled and they went in opposite directions, the women to the dance and José to his holdall.

They only met at meal times and Julia with her natural curiosity wanted to know what he did all day, so had enquired from her friend, the Catering Officer, but he was unable to help her and the intrigue continued.

It was on the second day that José had to inform them that he would not be coming in to dinner. This was startling news for Julia, so she wanted to know the reason.

When told that a passenger had complained that José was not dressed correctly for dinner as he did not wear a tie, her beautiful blue eyes sparkled with anger and being extremely outspoken, she swore, causing him to raise his eyebrows in consternation. She assured him he would have a tie before the evening and was as good as her word.

José had never met a more determined strong-willed woman before and he could feel warmth creeping through him. In his opinion, she was different from any woman he knew, amusing, intelligent, kind, unselfish and he was captivated by her.

Julia was enthralled with him and she found herself thinking of him at unexpected moments. How could she know that the same thing was happening to José.

Christmas day arrived with a flurry of excitement. Julia and Helen had unpacked their presents from their Australian friends and thought of them as they had promised.

It was Julia who was in a hurry to go to breakfast as she had bought a small gift for José, against her friend's advice. This she placed on his side plate and waited expectantly.

He was embarrassed by her kindness and mumbled his thanks. Realising his predicament she tried to make light of it but was puzzled by his attitude. The subject was changed and they talked about the forthcoming evening. Suddenly José dropped his bombshell. He could not attend dinner as he did not have a jacket.

Once again Julia became angry saying that it was a Christian Festival, why could people not behave accordingly. Surely it did not matter whether he had a jacket or not, as so often in the past when she had made similar outbursts on a multitude of injustices. It was Helen who reminded her that it was the custom on board ship and this rule had to be adhered to. Julia would not be outdone and her piercing blue eyes shone with suppressed anger as she thought out her plan of action. Then suddenly her face radiated happiness, of course, the problem was solved, she would borrow a jacket from her friend, the Catering Officer.

Later in the morning, José heard a knock on his cabin door and opening it he found the tall slim woman holding a coat hanger with a checked jacket, shirt and matching tie. He was overcome with an uncontrolled emotion, his eyes filled with tears. He could have hugged her but instead thanked her. Then the shock came when she asked him to take off his trousers. His face reddened with his embarrassment and he tightened his hold on them.

She, realizing the implication of her statement, burst into peals of laughter until the tears ran down her face. It was not a seduction.

The trousers were returned spotlessly clean with sharp creases in the legs that would have cut a few passenger's throats.

In the evening, José called for his two friends and escorted them to the Captain's Cocktail Party. As they entered the room, heads turned to look at one of the most handsome men on board.

Very soon, José was surrounded by women chatting, laughing and flirting with him but he never left his friends side. Julia was in her element, she had played her last trick and it had worked. She had little time for her travelling companions because they bored her silly. Now she stood on the edge of the crowd surveying them with contempt. Excusing himself from the bevy of beauties he escorted Julia and Helen into the restaurant. They stopped on the threshold and gasped with delight. It was like a magical cave, silver, reds, greens and golden coloured decorations were festooned around the room. The Christmas tree glittering in the light reminded them of icicles hanging from snow-capped trees after a severe frost. The two women felt a little home sick at that given moment. The tables were beautifully set with crackers, fresh fruit and the table cloths and napkins had festive motifs. Balloons held in a net, hung from the ceiling to be released later. This was an evening to be remembered forever.

As the wine waiter approached José, he announced that he would buy the wine and his two friends smiled their agreement. It was the last of his money, for tomorrow the ship would dock and he would be home.

When the meal ended, a dreadful silence descended. They were the only three people left in the restaurant and the time had come to say their goodbyes. Julia had tried encouraging him to go dancing with them but he had shaken his head. He was now completely without funds and his pride would not permit him to take any more hospitality.

Slowly removing the expensive jacket, he asked if he could personally thank their friend who had been so kind to him, only to be met with a positive "No." His large deep brown eyes were sad as he held Julia and kissed her gently on her lips. She held him to her for a few moments, as emotion overcame her, she pushed him away and taking the jacket from him, she walked blindly from the dining room. Helen shook his hand, wishing him success with his glass blowing and they parted company.

The next morning the two young women were up early on deck to look for José but he had left the ship which had anchored in the bay as the channel was too narrow and shallow for large ocean-going liners. They watched the passengers disembarking and travelling by motor launch to the harbour.

Later that morning they went sightseeing, taking pictures and walking, for what seemed hours, around the beautiful city. All sorts of little details and tourist items came under their delighted scrutiny. On their way back to the quayside they were surprised when a long black limousine, with drawn blinds, glided up beside them and a voice called their names. Julia and Helen glanced at each other before turning to the car. A well-dressed man in sunglasses stepped on to the pavement. They stared hard at him and he removed his sunglasses to reveal José grinning like a Cheshire Cat. Julia and Helen laughed spontaneously.

José entertained them in one of the most exclusive hotels in Acapulco. It was built into the side of a cliff, where one could sit and watch the high divers launching themselves from the heights into a narrow chasm where the ocean waves crashed on to the rocks.

José explained his circumstances over a magnificent dinner. Once more, he enquired who the kind man was who loaned him his clothing and once again he was refused. They accepted the three small packages from him, the third on behalf of the unknown officer.

He sighed as he waved farewell to his two dear friends and watched the launch with its occupants head towards the large liner. He had come on board the ship with a very heavy heart and had left it with a feeling of contentment. He had also learned that certain women can keep a secret!

Helen ran up the gangplank on to the ship but Julia stopped to wave to one of the most fascinating men she had the pleasure of meeting. She rested her arms on the rails and imagined the man who she had observed, what seemed like years ago, coming up the gangplank. She gave a farewell wave and a little sigh as she followed her friend Helen, who had gone in search of their friend, the Catering Officer. He was in the restaurant supervising his staff laying the tables for the morning breakfast and he looked up in surprise when the two young women arrived from their sightseeing tour. When they had not come in to dinner he had been perplexed but now he felt a sense of relief when he saw Helen's grinning face. Listening very carefully to Helen telling the story of their mystery man, he noticed that Julia had sat down at a nearby table and remained very quiet. She appeared to be miles away and he became a little concerned for her as he watched her. It was Helen who dragged him to the table and urged Julia to produce his present. Julia was startled out of her dream and he saw her face redden with embarrassment. Opening her handbag she handed José's present to him and he stared at it thoughtfully and then began un-wrapping the gift.

Helen, in her excitement, had begun ripping the paper off her gift and opened the small box which held a beautiful pair of diamond earrings. She held them up for all to admire.

Julia only gazed at them and without a word she began undoing her package. Opening the envelope which sat on top of her oblong box she began reading the hand written letter which began: My dear, dear, Julia. She blinked away her tears and read on. He thanked her for her Christmas present which was one gift that he had appreciated greatly. Then he went on to say that the enclosed cheque was for her and her friend to return to Acapulco for a holiday with his family. He had discussed with his family how wonderful she had been to him and they were insistent that he must invite her for a holiday but it was up to her to decide. He knew she had been hurt by his deception on board the ship but he had told her and her friend the truth that he was a Glassblower and that he was going to Acapulco to work. He did not think that they would have believed him if he had explained his circumstances and as far as he, at that time, was concerned had been the best way. After getting to know her so well, he realised that he had made a mistake and he hoped she would forgive him. The letter ended with him saying he hopes she accepts the cheque and visits soon. Julia was so full of emotion that her tears flowed down her face and dropped on to the paper, smudging the ink.

Helen, who had up until then, been talking non-stop, suddenly realised that her friend was upset. Her face showed her anxiety and she tried to make a joke of the presents but through her tears, Julia simply said that she was being silly. She passed her letter and cheque for a £1,000.00 over to Helen and then she concentrated on her gift.

Helen was amazed when she read the letter and started asking questions for which she received no answers as Julia was engaged in opening her oblong box. She gasped with shock when she saw the most gorgeous sparkling diamond necklace and, once again, she blinked back her tears. It was all too much for her.

The Catering Officer, in his understanding way, placed his hand over her hand and he did not say a word. He understood her feelings. When she looked up at him there was something in her eyes that pulled at the strings of his heart. He had never met a young woman who cared so much for humanity and he felt humbled.

Julia encouraged him to undo his present and he found a hand written note, written to the unknown friend, thanking him for being so kind and José hoping he would accept his gift. When he opened the small box he found a solid gold wristlet watch and he whistled his admiration and he passed it around to his friends. This was his first expensive present in many years and it was a gift that would always remind him of Julia. He could never refuse her odd requests for men's clothing but when he saw them on the man he had chuckled as he should have known. This was one trip he would never forget.

Julia could not understand why José had given them these expensive presents, for after all, she had only provided him with borrowed clothes.

The Catering Officer chuckled at her simplicity and asked her what was the Christmas present she had bought José.

She said simply, "Something he did not possess," and then added mischievously, "two pairs of socks."

The three friends burst out laughing and they laughed so hard that the catering staff stopped their work and joined in the merriment.